Sally Goes to the Mountains

Written and Illustrated by

Stephen Huneck

Harry N. Abrams, Inc., Publishers

Acknowledgments

I wish to thank my editor Howard Reeves and his assistant Lia Ronnen for their enthusiasm and commitment to Sally's newest adventure. I also wish to thank Chantel Amey and Mike Lamp for all their help in the studio. My deepest thanks to Jim and Lynn Bryant and Will Seippel for their friendship and support. And a special thank you to my wonderful wife Gwen for her encouragement and love.

Artist's Note

One of my greatest pleasures in life is taking all of my dogs for a walk in the deep forest on my farm "Dog Mountain" in St. Johnsbury, Vermont. The dogs become super alert and never go so far that they can't keep an eye on me. Sally has a funny thing that she does—she will sit down on the trail and wait for me to miss her. As soon as I call her she comes running. She likes to know I am always thinking of her—if she only knew!

To create a woodcut print, I first draw the design of the future print in crayon, laying out the prospective shapes and colors. I then carve one block of wood for each color in the appropriate shape. The result is a series of carved blocks, one for each color in the print. After a block has been inked with its respective color, acid-free archival paper is laid onto the block and hand rubbed. I repeat the process for each color block. When this process is completed, I then hang the prints to dry. —S.H.

Designer: Ellen Nygaard Ford

The artwork for each picture is prepared with woodblock prints on paper.
The text is set in 24 point Huneck Regular.

You may visit Stephen Huneck's website at: www.huneck.com

Library of Congress Cataloging-in-Publication Data
Huneck, Stephen.
Sally goes to the mountains / written & illustrated
by Stephen Huneck.
p. cm.
Summary: Sally, a black Labrador retriever, is on her
way to go camping in the mountains.
ISBN 0-8109-4485-5
[1. Dogs—Fiction. 2. Camping—Fiction.] I. Title.
PZ7.H8995 Sal 2001
[E]—dc21 00-42153

Printed and bound in Hong Kong

Harry N. Abrams, Inc.
100 Fifth Avenue
New York, N.Y. 10011
www.abramsbooks.com

To dogs everywhere
and the children who love them.

We are going camping in the mountains.
We read about the animals that live there.
I cannot wait to see them.

We load the van with our gear and lots of food.

"Sally, go to sleep. We will be there in the morning."

The mountains are beautiful

and hopping with life.

I want to play with a rabbit,

but he vanishes into thin air.

I climb a tree and meet a bird.

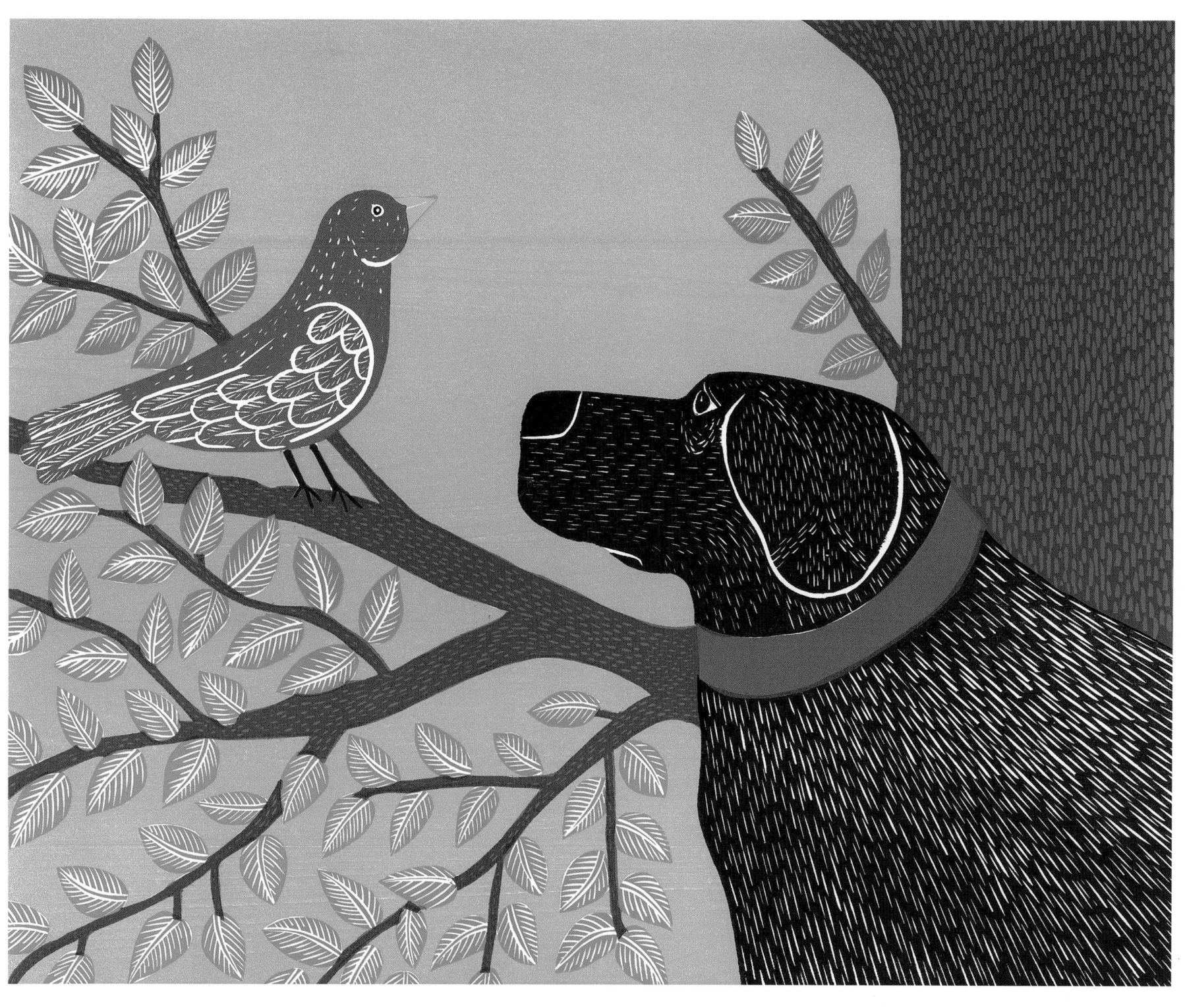

She sings a lovely song.

"Hi! My name is Sally." "Who?" "Sally." "Who?"

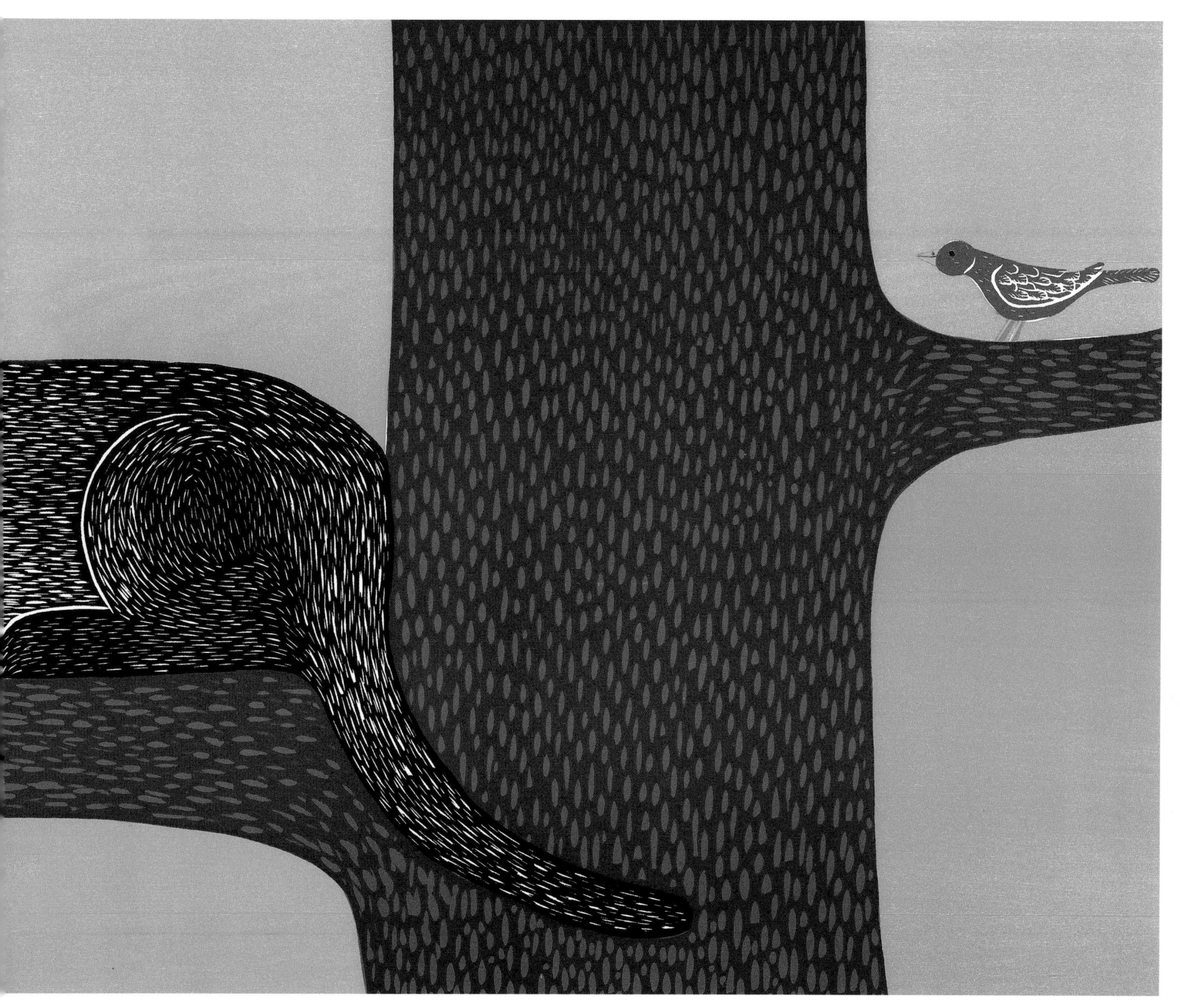

"Sally." "Who?" "Sally." "Who?" "Sally." "Who?"

I soon have enough of that.

I go for a swim.

The water is perfect,

and the fish are jumping.

I like sticks,

but the beaver has me beat.

A family of skunks is very nice,

except for one little stinker.

I want to play with a raccoon,

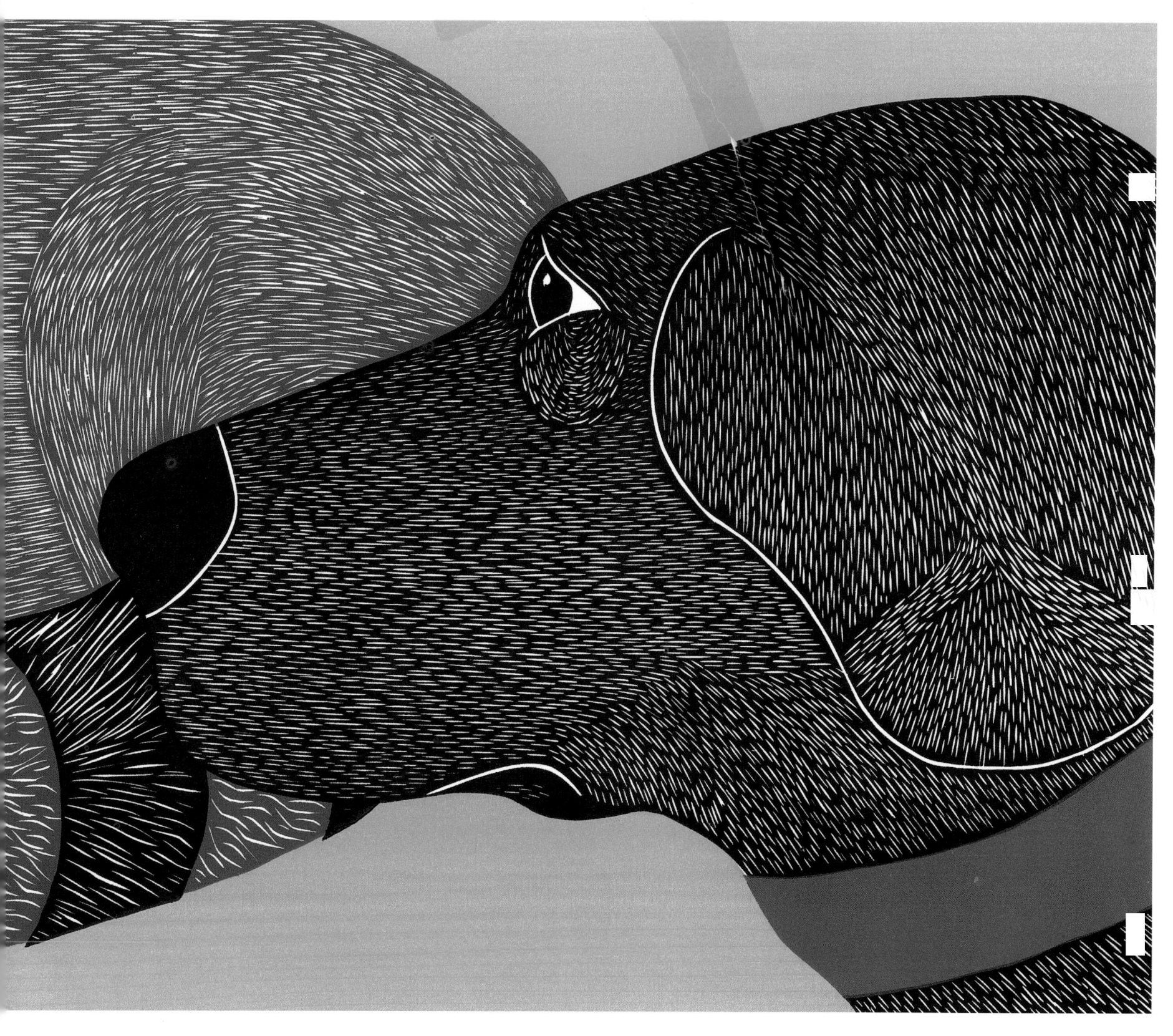

but he says, "Nighttime is playtime for me."

I see moose tracks all around . . .

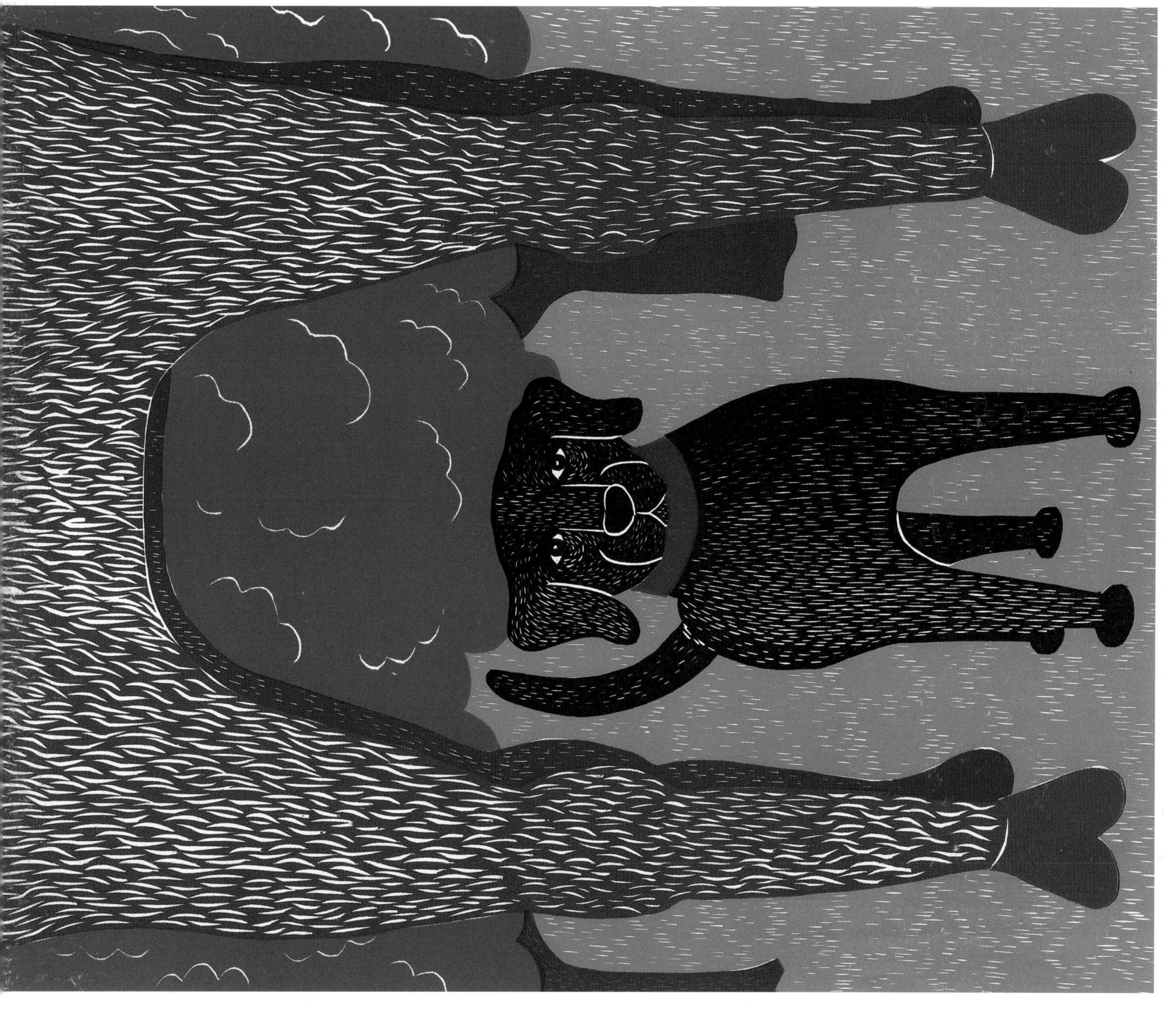

but I do not see a moose.

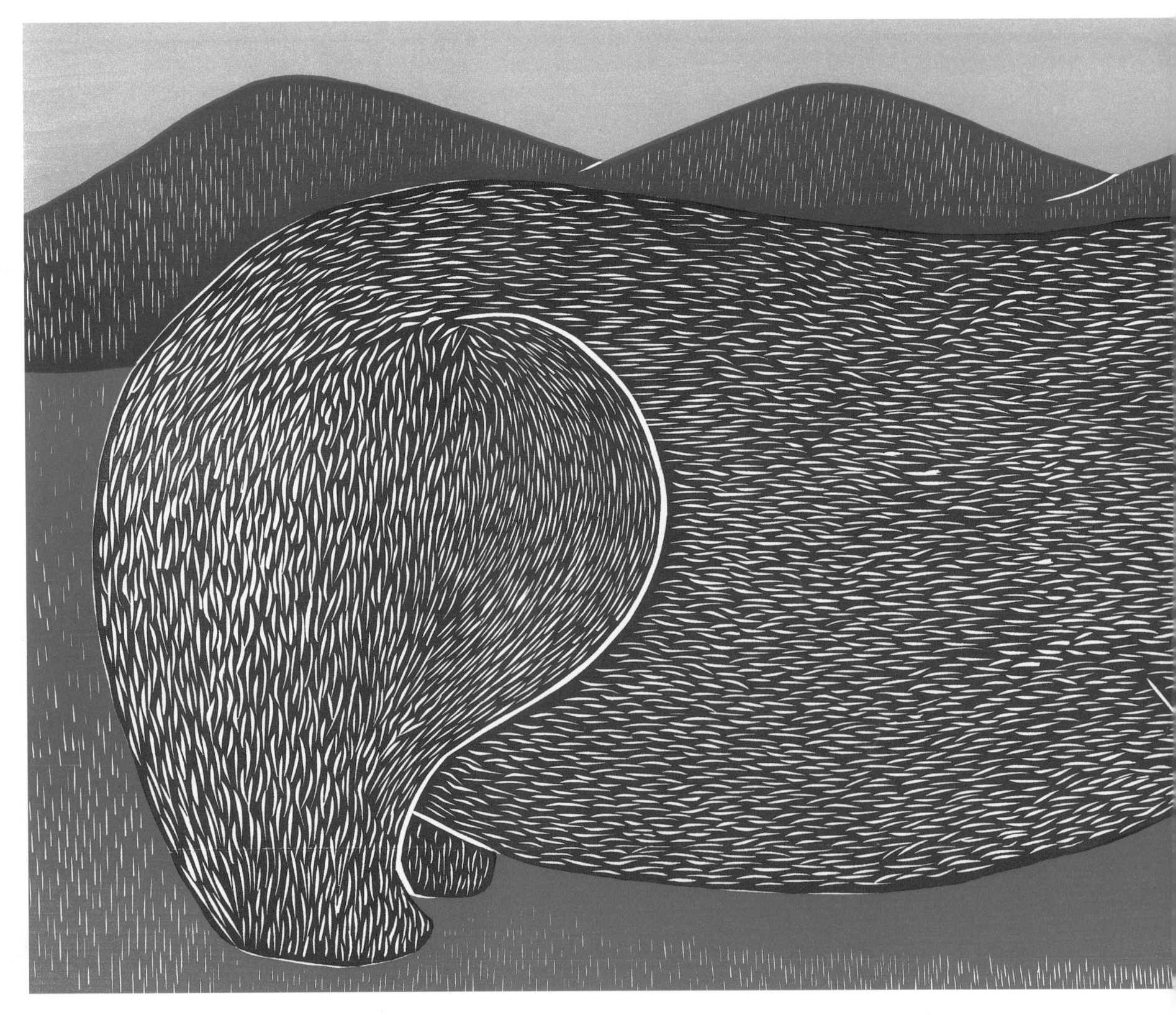

I meet a bear eating berries off a bush.

My stomach starts to growl.

I find a bush with my favorite food,
but no one to open the cans.

I have never been so hungry!

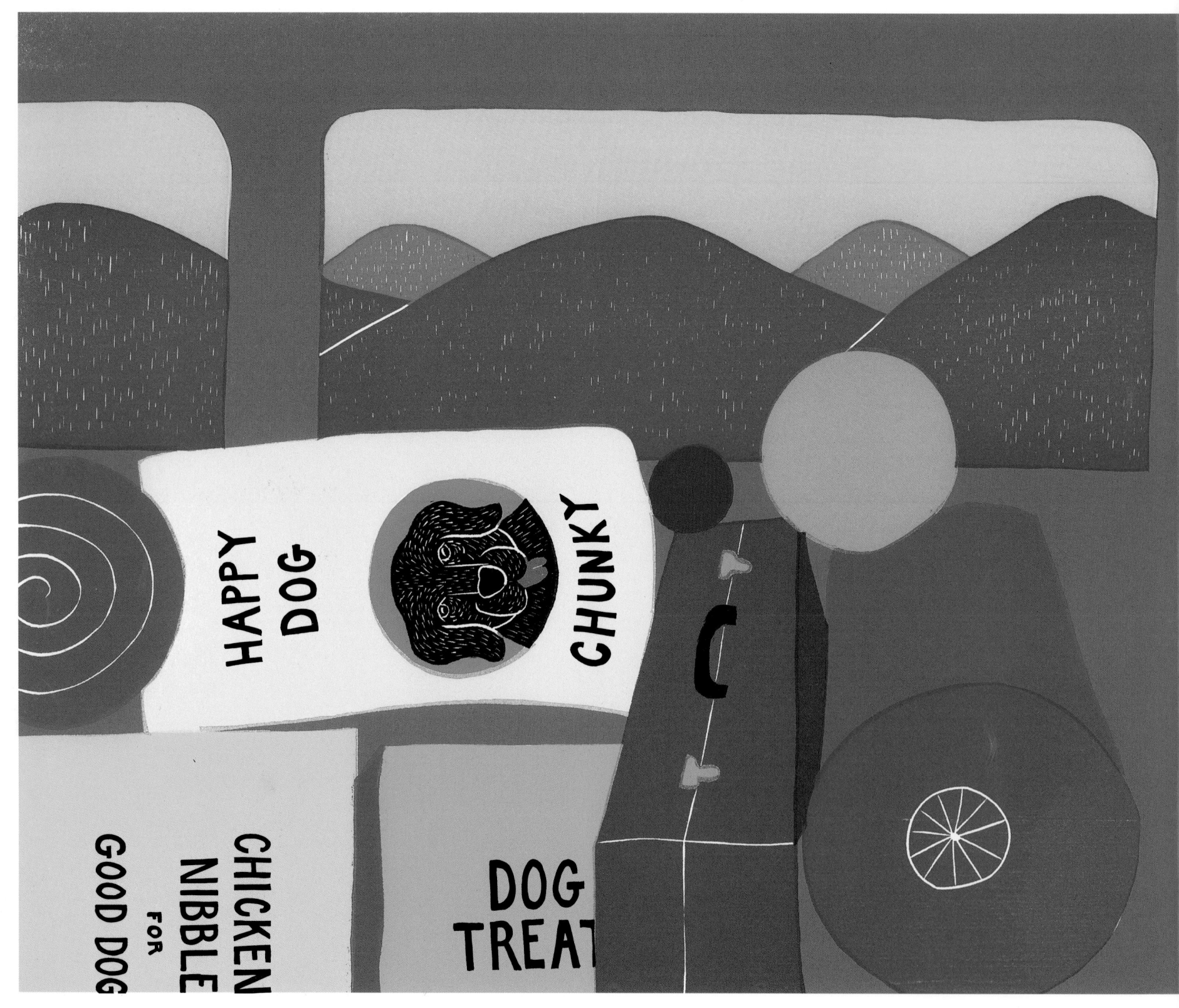

"Sally, wake up. We are in the mountains.

Time for breakfast!"